The King's Pyjamas

*For George, India, Isaac,
Matilda and Nicholas* – P.C.

For Matthew – C.C.

First published in Great Britain in 2001 by

⊘ Belitha Press Limited,
London House, Great Eastern Wharf
Parkgate Road, London SW11 4NQ

Copyright © Belitha Press Limited 2001
Illustration copyright © Christopher Corr

Series editor: Mary-Jane Wilkins
Editors: Stephanie Turnbull, Russell McLean
Designer: Sarah Goodwin
Illustrator: Christopher Corr

ISBN 1 84138 255 8

British Library Cataloguing in Publication Data for
this book is available from the British Library.

Printed in China

10 9 8 7 6 5 4 3 2 1

The King's Pyjamas

Compiled by Pie Corbett
Illustrated by Christopher Corr

Belitha Press

Contents

MY FRIENDS AND FAMILY

Un-Stable Auntie

My Auntie Josephine is mad.
She thinks she is a horse!
She eats huge plates of oats and hay
with heaps of chocolate sauce.

She trots around the dining room,
and canters up the stairs.
She loves to practise jumping
over lines of kitchen chairs.

On Sundays, at the racetrack,
she flicks her tail and grins.
But once she starts to gallop
my Auntie *always* wins!

Andrea Shavick

How to Get Your Granny out of Bed

You can open the curtains;
Switch on the light;
Pull back the covers;
Start a pillow fight;
Promise her a party
In the middle of the night
But
You won't get your granny out of bed.

You can let the dog lick her;
Try tickling her toes;
Stick a steaming cup of tea
Underneath her nose;
Hire a *Vogue* photographer
And ask her to pose
But
You won't get your granny out of bed.

You can find her a football strip
That fits like a dream;
Say you'll make her Captain
Of the town's top team,
Then she'll sit up and purr
Like the cat that got the cream:
Yes,
That'll get your granny out of bed.

Celia Warren

Jemima

Running down the garden path
Jemima seven years old
Lifts her eyes to watch the sun
Drown in clouds of gold.
Sees her old friend smiling down
Through the chestnut tree
Her round face in the branches shines
White as ivory.
Jemima tells her secrets
Her breath is like a sigh
Then makes a wish upon a star
That swoops across the sky.
Jemima up the garden path
The evening bright as noon
Tells anyone who'll listen,
'I've been talking to the moon.'

Gareth Owen

8

My Little Sister

They said they'd let me
hold her in the garden
for a photograph.

'Be careful,' they said.
'She's new and tiny
and very very precious.'

They sat me on a chair,
my legs dangling.
'Ready now?' they asked.

And they placed her
on my lap, wriggling and wet.
'Smile,' they said.

I tried, but it wasn't easy
to hold the baby and smile,
both at the same time.

Moira Andrew

9

Reflections

In my mirror
I often see
someone who
looks just like me!

He never seems
to brush his hair,
he dresses in
my underwear.

He must be shy
because he hides
whenever I
look round the sides.

I wish he would
come out to play.
Whatever does
he do all day?

Jane Clarke

10

Don't

Why do people say 'don't' so much,
Whenever you try something new?
It's more fun doing the don'ting,
So why don't people say 'do'?

Don't slurp your spaghetti
Don't kiss the cat
Don't butter your fingers
Don't walk like that
Don't wash your books
Don't bubble your tea
Don't jump on your sister
Don't goggle at me
Don't climb up the curtains
Don't feed the chair
Don't sleep in your wardrobe
Don't cut off your hair
Don't draw on the pillow
Don't change all the clocks
Don't water the phone
Don't hide my socks
Don't cycle upstairs
Don't write on the eggs
Don't chew your pyjamas
Don't paint your legs…

Oh, why do people say 'don't' so much,
Whenever you try something new?
It's more fun doing the don'ting,
So why don't people say 'do'?

Richard Edwards

I Hated Everyone Today

I hated everyone today.
I took a boat and sailed away,
I found an island in the sea
And there was nobody but me;
It had a little wooden hut,
A palm tree and a coconut.

I walked upon the silver shore,
I met a red and blue macaw.
The tales he told of pirates bold,
Of brigantines and Spanish gold,
Of Captain Blood and Captain Kidd
And all the dreadful deeds they did!

They plundered, pillaged, smoked and drank,
They made their prisoners walk the plank —
You reach the end and then you drop;
It makes a horrid kind of plop.
The seas around for miles and miles
Were thick with happy crocodiles.

At night beneath the tropic moon
We swam across the lost lagoon
Where seals and phosphorescent fish
Shimmered like a Christmas wish.
I did exactly as I chose
And nobody got up my nose.

John Whitworth

Favouritism

When we caught measles
It wasn't fair —
My brother collected
Twice his share.

He counted my spots:
'One hundred and twenty!'
Which sounded to me
As if I had plenty.

Then I counted his —
And what do you think?
He'd two hundred and thirty-eight,
Small, round and pink!

I felt I'd been cheated
So 'Count mine again!'
I told him, and scowled
So he dared not complain.

'One hundred and twenty' —
The same as before…
In our house, he's youngest
And he always gets more!

Trevor Harvey

Don't be Such a Fusspot

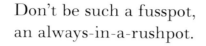

Don't be such a fusspot,
an always-in-a-rushpot.

Don't be such a weepypot,
a sneak-to-mum-and-be-creepypot.

Don't be such a muddlepot,
a double-dose-of-troublepot.

Don't be such a wigglepot,
a sit-on-your-seat-don't-squigglepot.

Don't be such a muckypot,
a pick-up-slugs-and-be-yuckypot.

Don't be such a sleepypot,
a beneath-the-bedclothes-peepypot.

Don't be such a fiddlepot,
a mess-about-and-meddlepot.

Don't be such a bossypot,
a saucypot, a gigglepot,
don't be such a lazypot,
a nigglepot, a slackpot.

And don't call me a crackpot…
Who do you think you are?

Brian Moses

Family Hobbies

Brother Bart?
Likes art
Sister Hayley?
Ukulele
Dad?
Football mad
Mum?
A rugby scrum
Auntie Rose?
Sewing clothes
Uncle Sly?
DIY
Gramps?
Collecting stamps
Granny?
Playing her tranny
Great-grandad Marcel?
Miming
And my hobby is?

Roger Stevens

Every Child's Answer

to that telephone query from a distant relative...

'Are you growing up fast?'

> 'Yes, I've just hit the ceiling.
> Now I've gone through the roof
> And at present I'm kneeling
> To hear what you're saying,
> With my legs through the door,
> One arm through the window,
> My chin on the floor
> And my feet in the roadway,
> Which are causing a worry
> With a traffic jam stretching
> For ten miles through Surrey…
>
> So I'd better ring off…
>
> 'Bye!'

Trevor Harvey

Squeezes

We love to squeeze bananas,
We love to squeeze ripe plums,
And when they are feeling sad
We love to squeeze our mums.

Brian Patten

How Many Make a Family?

How many make a family?
My friend Joe says five:
His mum, his dad, his sister, him,
And little brother Clive.

But Sophie's got a granny,
An uncle, Cousin Ben,
Brothers, sisters, mum and dad –
She thinks it comes to ten.

Sadie says it must be six,
Sammy says it's three,
But I say that it's two because
There's only mum and me.

So I asked mum the question,
As she tucked me into bed,
'How many make a family?'
And this is what she said:

'A family's to share with –
Our home, our life, our love.
So it really doesn't matter –
Any number is enough!'

Sue Palmer

TIME FOR SCHOOL

The Great Teacher Mystery

What happens to our teachers
When we go home each day?
Do they put their trainers on
And skip outside to play?

Do they eat chalk sandwiches
With plasticine for tea?
Do they sit up much too late
And watch the school TV?

Do they keep their slippers
And pyjamas hung on hooks?
Do they sleep in cupboards
With the pencils and the books?

Do they have to bath themselves
Squashed up inside the sinks?
Do they? Yes, of course they do –
That's what my best friend thinks.

Clare Bevan

Our Teacher

Our teacher is a hamster
Don't be surprised by that.
Yesterday he was a goat
And the day before a bat.

He started out as a human being
For the first few days of term
But since then he's been lots of things
From a puppy to a worm.

He's also been a rabbit
A parrot and a mole
He's taught us sitting on a perch
And burrowed down a hole.

It can be quite confusing
And sometimes we forget
That he really is a teacher
And we treat him like a pet.

John Coldwell

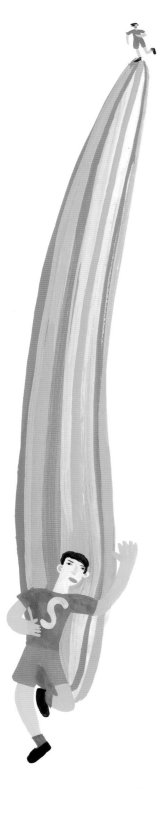

Little Danny

Little Danny had no muscles,
Didn't seem the sort for tussles.

Other kids said, 'Look at him,
He's so skinny, he's so thin,
Couldn't lift a bag of air,
Couldn't fight a teddy bear.'

BUT

When the Bully Boys came by,
Little Danny winked his eye,
Then I'll tell you what he did –
Turned into The Super Kid!

Zoomed across the crowded yard,
Zapped the Bully Boys SO hard
All of them ran home in tears
While the playground rang with cheers.

MORAL:

Don't judge people by their sizes –
Life is full of BIG surprises.

Clare Bevan

Picking Teams

When we pick teams in the playground,
Whatever the game might be,
There's always somebody left till last
And usually it's me.

I stand there looking hopeful
And tapping myself on the chest,
But the captains pick the others first,
Starting, of course, with the best.

Maybe if teams were sometimes picked
Starting with the worst,
Once in his life a boy like me
Could end up being first!

Allan Ahlberg

Down by the School Gate

There goes the bell
it's half past three
and down by the school gate
you will see…

…ten mums talk talk talking
nine babies squawk squawking
eight toddlers all squabbling
seven grans on bikes wobbling

six dogs bark bark barking
five cars stopping, parking
four child-minders running
three bus drivers sunning

two teenagers dating
one lollipop man waiting…

The school is out,
it's half past three
and the first to the school gate
…is me!

Wes Magee

Freddie Phipps

Freddie Phipps
Liked fish and chips.
Jesse Pinch liked crime.

Woodrow Waters
Liked dollars and quarters.
Paul Small liked a dime.

Sammy Fink
Liked a lemon drink.
Jeremy Jones liked lime.

Mortimer Mills
Liked running down hills.
Jack Jay liked to climb.

Hamilton Hope
Liked water and soap.
Georgie Green liked grime;

But Willy Earls
Liked pretty girls
And had a much better time.

Charles Causley

HOLIDAY FUN

Oh, Take Me to the Seaside!

Oh, take me to the seaside
On a day just like today
To smell the tang of seaweed,
Feel the stinging of the spray,
To see the breakers, taste the salt
And hear the crash of foam —
Please take me to the seaside
Then forget to take me home!

Sue Cowling

Revenge

My brother chased me with a crab,
He found it by a rock,
But I WILL get my own back —
It's now inside his sock!

Coral Rumble

What's in Our Luggage?

Wellies in case it rains,
sunhat for when it's hot,
net for going fishing —
I hope we catch a lot!

Bikes on the roof rack,
bucket and spade for the beach,
marshmallows for toasting —
at least three packets each!

Plasters (I'm bound to fall over!)
sunglasses for when it's bright,
toothbrush (Mum said so),
teddy to cuddle at night.

Picnic on the dashboard
ready for our tea...
so much luggage *everywhere*
there's no room left for *me*!

Tracey Blance

Round and round the rugged rocks the ragged rascal ran.

The Engine Driver

The train goes running along the line,
    Jicketty-can, jicketty-can.
I wish it were mine, I wish it were mine,
    Jicketty-can, jicketty-can.
The engine driver stands in front –
    He makes it run, he makes it shunt.

    Out of the town,
    Out of the town,
    Over the hill,
    Over the down,
    Under the bridges,
    Across the lea,
    Over the ridges
    And down to the sea.

With a jicketty-can, jicketty-can,
Jicketty-jicketty-jicketty-can,
Jicketty-can, jicketty-can…

Clive Sansom

Helter-Skelter

On my mat of coconut
whizzing round and round
trailing streams of corkscrew screams
till we reach the ground.

Gina Douthwaite

Ice Lolly

Red rocket
on a stick.
If it shines,
lick it quick.

Round the edges,
on the top,
round the bottom,
do not stop.

Suck the lolly.
Lick your lips.
Lick the sides
as it drips

off the stick —
quick, quick,
lick, lick —
Red rocket
on a stick.

Pie Corbett

Snow-Cone

Snow-cone nice
Snow-cone sweet
Snow-cone is crush ice
and good for the heat.

When sun really hot
and I thirsty a lot,
Me alone,
Yes me alone,
could eat ten snow-cone.
If you think is lie I tell

wait till you hear the snow-cone bell,
wait till you hear the snow-cone bell.

John Agard

RHYMES AND SILLY STUFF

Oranges and Lemons

Oranges and lemons,
Say the bells of St Clement's.

Pancakes and fritters,
Say the bells of St Peter's.

Two sticks and an apple,
Say the bells at Whitechapel.

Old Father Baldpate,
Say the slow bells at Aldgate.

Pokers and tongs,
Say the bells at St John's.

Kettles and pans,
Say the bells at St Ann's.

You owe me five farthings,
Say the bells at St Martin's.

When will you pay me?
Say the bells at Old Bailey.

When I grow rich,
Say the bells at Shoreditch.

Pray when will that be?
Say the bells of Stepney.

I'm sure I don't know,
Says the great bell at Bow.

Here comes a candle to light you to bed,
And here comes a chopper to chop off your head.
Last, last, last, last, last man's head.

Anon

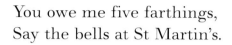

I Said My Pyjamas

I said my pyjamas,
I slipped on my prayers.
I went up my slippers,
I took off the stairs.
I turned off the bed,
I jumped in the light.
The reason for this…
You gave me a fright!

Anon

The Boy Stood on
the Burning Deck

The boy stood on the burning deck,
His feet were full of blisters.
The flames came up and burned his pants,
So now he wears his sister's.

Anon

36

Humpty Dumpty

Humpty Dumpty sat on a wall,
Eating green bananas.
Where do you think he put the skins?
Down the King's pyjamas!

Anon

Little Miss Muffet

Little Miss Muffet
Sat on a tuffet,
Eating some Irish stew.
There came a big spider
That sat down beside her
And so she ate him up too.

Anon

37

My Name Is...

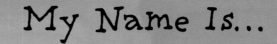

My name is Sluggery-wuggery
My name is Worms-for-tea
My name is Swallow-the-table-leg
My name is Drink-the-Sea
My name is I-eat-saucepans
My name is I-like-snails
My name is Grand-piano-George
My name is I-ride-whales.
My name is Jump-the-chimney
My name is Bite-my-knee
My name is Jiggery-pokery
And Riddle-me-ree,
and me

Pauline Clarke

What Am I?

Nursery-rhyme boat
afloat in the night.
A cheesy grin,
in a ghostly white.
A silver face,
in an icy night.

Pie Corbett

Well, I Never!

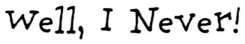

The other day I swallowed a pig,
It was ever so big,
The other day I swallowed a goat,
It slid down my throat,
The other day I swallowed a farm,
I came to no harm,
The other day I swallowed a bull,
I was really full,
The other day I swallowed a horse,
Delicious, of course,
And only last week I swallowed a hen,
I'm not sure when,
The other day I swallowed my pride,
And was sorry I lied
About the pig and the goat,
    the farm and the bull,
    the horse and the hen,
So I started again…

The other day I swallowed a tooth –
    Now, that's the truth!

June Crebbin

At King Neptune's Party

At King Neptune's party
The whales had a whale of a time.
The octopus did the eightsome reel.
The sea slug slithered in slime.

The sea horse pranced. The dolphins danced.
The seals performed their tricks.
The eels wriggled. The jellyfish giggled.
The snapper took lots of pics.

The mermaids let their hair down.
The sea lion gave a roar.
The porpoise played. The swordfish swayed.
The crabs all waved a claw.

Flying fish did aerobatics.
The turtles did the twist.
Tuna played tunes. Oysters swooned.
Lobsters blushed and kissed.

At King Neptune's party
The whales had a whale of a time.
The octopus did the eightsome reel.
The sea slug slithered in slime.

John Foster

40

Pies

I spied a pie through the baker's door
And then I spied a whole lot more

Apple pie with crusty topping
Rabbit pie that won't stop hopping
Mince pie hot on Christmas Day
Pigeon pie that flies away
Cottage pie with bricks and mortar
Octopi found underwater
Butcher's pie with steak and kidney
Witch's pie with Kate and Sidney
Shepherd's pie with spuds and carrots
Pirate's pie with squawking parrots
Blackbird pie begins to sing
Eel pie keeps on wriggling
Custard pie that someone throws
Mud pie oozing through your toes
Fish pie swimming in the sea
Cherry pie — the one for me!

I spied a pie through the baker's door
A spider pie? Are you really sure?

Paul Bright

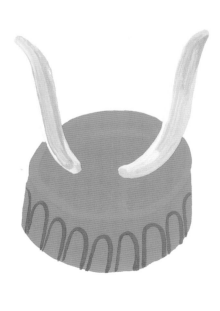

41

ANIMAL ALLSORTS

Cat walking Across the Grass

It's
a
ginger

sun in
a

green
sky

ears pushed

back

head

held

high

Ian McMillan

Cat

White as spun silk
the moon looks down.
Babs my cat looks back
and ponders the leap.

Brian Morse

Ginger Tom

He'll watch TV
If there's a programme on fishing
With eyes agleam
And striped tail swishing,
Devising
A cunning scheme

But he's scared of wetting
His marmalade coat
And he wouldn't go out
With an owl in a boat
If you paid him
In double cream!

Sue Cowling

The Owl and the Pussy-Cat

The Owl and the Pussy-Cat went to sea
  In a beautiful pea-green boat,
They took some honey, and plenty of money,
  Wrapped up in a five-pound note.
The Owl looked up to the stars above,
  And sang to a small guitar,
'O lovely Pussy! O Pussy, my love,
  What a beautiful Pussy you are,
    You are,
    You are!
  What a beautiful Pussy you are!'

Pussy said to the Owl, 'You elegant fowl!
  How charmingly sweet you sing!
O let us be married! too long have we tarried:
  But what shall we do for a ring?'
They sailed away, for a year and a day,
  To the land where the Bong-tree grows
And there in a wood a Piggy-wig stood
  With a ring at the end of his nose,
    His nose,
    His nose,
  With a ring at the end of his nose.

'Dear Pig, are you willing to sell for one shilling
    Your ring?' Said the Piggy, 'I will.'
So they took it away, and were married next day
    By the Turkey who lives on the hill.
They dined on mince, and slices of quince,
    Which they ate with a runcible spoon;
And hand in hand, on the edge of the sand,
    They danced by the light of the moon,
        The moon,
        The moon,
    They danced by the light of the moon.

Edward Lear

Cow

The cow
Coming
Across the grass
Moves
Like a mountain
Towards us;
Her hipbones
Jut
Like sharp
Peaks
Of stone,
Her hoofs
Thump
Like dropped
Rocks:
Almost
Too late
She stops.

Valerie Worth

Milking Time

Five o'clock in the morning
cows cross the dark yard
like white patches of jigsaw,
their hot breath making misty ghosts
in the crisp air.

Gina Douthwaite

Pigeon-watch

The pigeon struts
along the ledge:
he never gets
too near the edge.

Katherine Gallagher

Porch Light

At night
  the porch light
    catches moths
     and holds them,
     trapped
    and
     flapping,
    in a tight
    yellow fist.
    Only when I
   turn the switch
   will it loosen
  its
  grip.

Deborah Chandra

Roger was a Razor Fish

Roger was a razor fish
as sharp as he could be.
He said to Calvin Catfish
'I'll shave you for a fee.'

'No thanks,'
said Calvin Catfish.
'I like me like I be.'
And with his whiskers
on his face
he headed out to sea.

Al Pittman

50

I Wannabe a Wallaby

I wannabe a wallaby,
A wallaby that's true.
Don't wannabe a possum
A koala or a roo.

I wannago hop hopping
Anywhere I please.
Hopping without stopping
Through eucalyptus trees.

A wallaby, a wallaby
Is what I wannabe.
I'd swap my life to be one,
But a problem — I can see;

If I'm gonna be a wallaby
I shall have to go and see
If I can find a wallaby,
A very friendly wallaby,
Who would really, really, really…

Wannabe… ME!

David Whitehead

The Dinosaur's Dinner

Once a mighty dinosaur
Came to dine with me,
He gobbled up the curtains
And swallowed our settee.

He didn't seem to fancy
Onion soup with crusty bread,
He much preferred the flavour
Of our furniture instead.

He ate up all our dining-chairs
And carpets from the floor,
He polished off the table, then
He looked around for more.

The television disappeared
In one almighty gulp,
Wardrobes, beds and bathroom
He crunched into a pulp.

He really loved the greenhouse,
He liked the garden shed,
He started on the chimney-pots
But then my mother said:

'Your friends are always welcome
To drop in for a bite,
But really this one seems to have
A giant appetite.

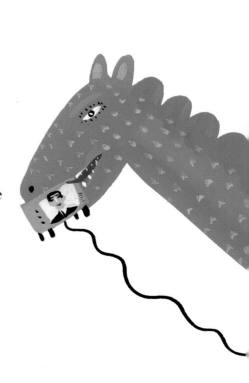

You'd better take him somewhere else,
I'm sure I don't know where,
I only know this friend of yours
Needs more than we can spare!'

And suddenly I realized
I knew the very place,
And when I showed him where it was
You should have seen his face —

I don't think I've seen anyone
Enjoy a dinner more,
I watched him wander on his way,
A happy dinosaur!

The council did rebuild our school,
But that of course took time…
And all because a dinosaur
Came home with me to dine!

June Crebbin

WEATHER AND WONDER
It's Spring

It's spring
And the garden is changing its clothes,
Putting away
Its dark winter suits,
Its dull scarves
And drab brown overcoats.

Now, it wraps itself in green shoots,
Slips on blouses
Sleeved with pink and white blossom,
Pulls on skirts of daffodil and primrose,
Snowdrop socks and purple crocus shoes,
Then dances in the sunlight.

John Foster

A Ragged Band

The wind at night's
a tin can kicked round by a team of ghostly children,
an ocean wave roaring one end of the street to the other,
a skeleton's teeth chattering with cold,
a scarecrow's nightmare,
a drunken herd of elephants,
a bag of bones clattering around the yard,
a line of trees dancing an Irish jig!

It's
a moon-scolding cat,
an out-of-sorts drummer,
a gang of ghosts out for a bone-rattle,
a squall of hissing snakes,
a vicious kitten clawing the house fronts,
a thief testing all the windows,
the End Of All Time Orchestra!

Brian Morse

Silver

Silver for the tiny tooth
Hidden under pillow;
Silver for the shining knife;
Silver leaf on willow;
Silver coin in pudding;
Satin-silver dish;
Silver face of midnight moon;
Silvery, slippery fish;
Silver sheen of trumpet;
Silver fox at play;
Silver threads in Grandma's hair
At ending of the day.

John Kitching

Starry

Hey the starry night-time
  and its starry plain,
starry is the silence
  of its starry train.
Starry are the curtains,
  starry wall and door,
starry falls the starlight
  on my starry floor.

Hey the starry night-time
  and its starry glow,
starry is the window
  with the starry show.
Starry are the colours
  starry blue and red,
starry falls the starlight
  on my starry bed.

John Rice

57

Last Night it Froze

There are ferns of frost on the window pane
And ice on the puddles in the lane.

Tufts of grass stick up like spikes.
It's far too slippery to ride our bikes.

Icicles hang like spears from the gutters.
The car engine whines and coughs and splutters.

The leaves on the trees are stiff and white.
While we slept, it froze last night.

John Foster

The Sweeper in the Snowy Street

Snow fell silent in the night
and now the street is frosty white.

I watch a man with snowy feet
go slowly sweeping down the street.

His heavy boots have ice-capped toes.
An icicle hangs from his nose.

Fresh-scarfed with snow he seems so old,
this lonely figure in the cold.

Beneath a chilled and greylag sky
he sweeps and sweeps as snowflakes fly.

Along the street I watch him go,
a snowman sweeping in the snow.

Wes Magee

Drum

Played softly:
a badger's heartbeat,
mountain river,
tumbling.

Played louder:
soldiers marching,
giant's tummy,
rumbling.

Played loudest:
roll of thunder,
black volcano
grumbling.

Judith Nicholls

Water

Water, water everywhere
And far too much to drink:
Water in the bath-tub;
Water in the sink;
Water in my coffee;
Water in your tea;
Water in the rain-storm;
Water in the sea;
Water in the rivers
Running through the land.

So why are children thirsty
In that dry and desert land?

John Kitching

End Poem

By hook —
   or by crook —
I am last
   in this book.

Anon

Index of titles and first lines

First lines are in italics

Index of authors

Acknowledgements

John Agard: 'Snow-Cone' from *I Din Do Nuttin* by John Agard, published by Bodley Head. Used by permission of the Random House Group Limited. **Allan Ahlberg**: 'Picking Teams' (p35, 12 lines) from *Please Mrs Butler* by Allan Ahlberg (Kestrel, 1983). Copyright © Allan Ahlberg, 1983. **Moira Andrew**: 'My Little Sister' © Moira Andrew, first published in *At Home and Next Door*, ed. Robyn Gordon (Riverpoint Publishing, 1998). **Clare Bevan**: 'The Great Teacher Mystery' and 'Little Danny' © Clare Bevan, by permission of the author. **Tracey Blance**: 'What's in Our Luggage?' © Tracey Blance, by permission of the author. **Paul Bright**: 'Pies' © Paul Bright, by permission of the author. **Charles Causley**: 'Freddie Phipps' from *Early in the Morning* by Charles Causley, published by Penguin. **Deborah Chandra**: 'Porch Light' from *Balloons and Other Poems* by Deborah Chandra. Copyright © 1990 by Deborah Chandra. Reprinted by permission of Farrar, Straus and Giroux, LLC. **Jane Clarke**: 'Reflections' © Jane Clarke, by permission of the author. **Pauline Clarke**: 'My Name Is...' from *Silver Bells and Cockle Shells* © Pauline Clarke 1962, reproduced by permission of Curtis Brown, London. **John Coldwell**: 'Our Teacher' © John Coldwell, by permission of the author. **Pie Corbett**: 'Ice Lolly' and 'What Am I?' © Pie Corbett, by permission of the author. **Sue Cowling**: 'Oh, Take Me to the Seaside!' and 'Ginger Tom' © Sue Cowling, by permission of the author. **June Crebbin**: 'The Dinosaur's Dinner' from *The Dinosaur's Dinner* (Viking, 1992) © June Crebbin, by permission of the author. 'Well, I Never!' (p34, 20 lines) from *Cows Moo, Cars Toot!* by June Crebbin (Viking, 1995). Copyright © June Crebbin, 1995. **Gina Douthwaite**: 'Helter-Skelter' © Gina Douthwaite, from *Whizz-Bang Orang-Utan* (Oxford, 1999); 'Milking Time' © Gina Douthwaite; both included by permission of the author. **Richard Edwards**: 'Don't' by permission of the author (from *The Word Party*, published by Lutterworth, 1986). **John Foster**: 'At King Neptune's Party' © 2001 John Foster, from *Word Wizard* (Oxford University Press); 'It's Spring' © 1995 John Foster, from *Standing on the Sidelines* (Oxford University Press); 'Last Night it Froze' © 2000 John Foster, from *Climb Aboard the Poetry Plane* (Oxford University Press); all included by permission of the author. **Katherine Gallagher**: 'Pigeon-Watch' © Katherine Gallagher, by permission of the author. **Trevor Harvey**: 'Every Child's Answer' © Trevor Harvey, first published in *Read a Poem, Write a Poem*, ed. Wes Magee (Blackwell, 1989); 'Favouritism' © Trevor Harvey, first published in *Poetry for Projects*, ed. Brian Moses and Pie Corbett (Scholastic, 1989); both included by permission of the author. **John Kitching**: 'Silver' and 'Water' © John Kitching, by permission of the author. **Wes Magee**: 'Down by the School Gate' and 'The Sweeper in the Snowy Street' © Wes Magee, by permission of the author. **Ian McMillan**: 'Cat Walking Across the Grass' © Ian McMillan, by permission of the author. **Brian Morse**: 'Cat' and 'A Ragged Band' © Brian Morse, by permission of the author. **Brian Moses**: 'Don't be Such a Fusspot' © Brian Moses, by permission of the author. **Judith Nicholls**: 'Drum' © Judith Nicholls, by permission of the author. **Gareth Owen**: 'Jemima'. Copyright © Gareth Owen 2001, reproduced by permission of the author c/o Rogers, Coleridge & White Ltd., 20 Powis Mews, London W11 1JN. **Sue Palmer**: 'How Many Make a Family?' © Sue Palmer, by permission of the author. **Brian Patten**: 'Squeezes' (p11, 4 lines) from *Gargling With Jelly* by Brian Patten (Viking, 1985). Copyright © Brian Patten, 1985. **Al Pittman**: 'Roger Was a Razor Fish' reproduced with the permission of Breakwater, © the author. **John Rice**: 'Starry' © John Rice, by permission of the author. **Coral Rumble**: 'Revenge' © Coral Rumble, by permission of the author. **Clive Sansom**: 'The Engine Driver' from *Speech Rhymes*, chosen by Clive Sansom, published by A & C Black Ltd. **Andrea Shavick**: 'Un-Stable Auntie' © Andrea Shavick, by permission of the author. **Roger Stevens**: 'Family Hobbies' © Roger Stevens, by permission of the author. **Celia Warren**: 'How to Get Your Granny out of Bed' © Celia Warren, by permission of the author. **David Whitehead**: 'I Wannabe a Wallaby' first published in *Animal Poems*, ed. Jennifer Curry (Scholastic Young Hippo) © David Whitehead, 1998. **John Whitworth**: 'I Hated Everyone Today' © John Whitworth, by permission of the author. **Valerie Worth**: 'Cow' from *All the Small Poems and Fourteen More* by Valerie Worth. Copyright © 1987, 1994 by Valerie Worth. Reprinted by permission of Farrar, Straus and Giroux, LLC.

Every effort has been made to contact copyright holders. The publishers would like to hear from any copyright holder not acknowledged.